Crayon Girl!

T0337339

Written by Jane Clarke

Illustrated by Lee Teng

Collins

What's in this story?

Listen and say

lamp

pencil case

Download the audio at www.collins.co.uk/839802

phone

crayon

Maya's family was in the living room. Everyone was on the phone.

Maya was bored. She wanted to draw. She looked for her pencil case.

There were coloured pencils and there was a big crayon in her pencil case.

What picture can I draw?

Maya drew *Crayon Girl.*

Crayon Girl had arms and legs ... and big boots on her feet.

Crayon Girl had lots of colours.

I can *zap, zap, zap!*

Crayon Girl had a family.
They were pencils. Their names were Red,
Green, Blue and Yellow.

Crayon Girl had a cat named Orange.

Maya had an idea. A comic book.
A *Crayon Girl* comic book.

Crayon Girl said, "Our pencil case is always open. We can see the lamp. We all love the lamp."

The Screen's big.

The Screen's very big.

The Screen's very, very big!

Where was the lamp? There was only
The Screen.

15

The pencil case family was safe again. They could see the lamp. They could read and they could draw again. Everyone was happy.

Maya put her pencils in the pencil case.
She showed her family her comic book.
Maya's family read the story and looked at the pictures.

Everyone loved the *Crayon Girl!* comic book.

Maya and her family were in the
living room. They all had an idea for
a comic book. They all wanted to draw.
There were no phones.
They drew and talked.

Everyone was happy. It was fun to draw a comic book!

Picture dictionary

Listen and repeat

comic book

crayon

family

lamp

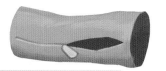
pencil case

phone

screen

1 Look and order the story

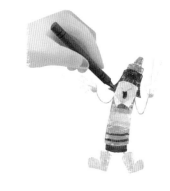

2 Listen and say

Download a reading guide for parents and teachers at
www.collins.co.uk/839802

Collins

Published by Collins
An imprint of HarperCollins*Publishers*
Westerhill Road
Bishopbriggs
Glasgow
G64 2QT

HarperCollins*Publishers*
1st Floor, Watermarque Building
Ringsend Road
Dublin 4
Ireland

William Collins' dream of knowledge for all began with the publication of his first book in 1819.

A self-educated mill worker, he not only enriched millions of lives, but also founded a flourishing publishing house. Today, staying true to this spirit, Collins books are packed with inspiration, innovation and practical expertise. They place you at the centre of a world of possibility and give you exactly what you need to explore it.

© HarperCollins*Publishers* Limited 2020

10 9 8 7 6 5 4 3 2

ISBN 978-0-00-839802-6

Collins® and COBUILD® are registered trademarks of HarperCollins*Publishers* Limited

www.collins.co.uk/elt

All rights reserved. No part of this publication may be reproduced, stored in a retrieval system, or transmitted in any form by any means, electronic, mechanical, photocopying, recording or otherwise, without the prior written permission of the Publisher or a licence permitting restricted copying in the United Kingdom issued by the Copyright Licensing Agency Ltd, 5th Floor, Shackleton House, 4 Battle Bridge Lane, London SE1 2HX.

British Library Cataloguing in Publication Data

A catalogue record for this publication is available from the British Library.

All rights reserved. No part of this book may be reproduced, stored in a retrieval system, or transmitted in any form or by any means, electronic, mechanical, photocopying, recording or otherwise, without the prior permission in writing of the Publisher. This book is sold subject to the conditions that it shall not, by way of trade or otherwise, be lent, re-sold, hired out or otherwise circulated without the Publisher's prior consent in any form of binding or cover other than that in which it is published and without a similar condition including this condition being imposed on the subsequent purchaser.

Author: Jane Clarke
Illustrator: Lee Teng (Beehive)
Series editor: Rebecca Adlard
Publishing manager: Lisa Todd
Product managers: Jennifer Hall and Caroline Green
In-house editor: Alma Puts Keren
Project manager: Emily Hooton
Editor: Frances Amrani
Proofreaders: Natalie Murray and Michael Lamb
Cover designer: Kevin Robbins
Typesetter: 2Hoots Publishing Services Ltd
Audio produced by id audio, London
Reading guide author: Matthew Hancock
Production controller: Rachel Weaver
Printed and bound by: GPS Group, Slovenia

MIX
Paper from
responsible sources
FSC www.fsc.org **FSC** C007454

This book is produced from independently certified FSC™ paper to ensure responsible forest management.

For more information visit: **www.harpercollins.co.uk/green**

Download the audio for this book and a reading guide for parents and teachers at www.collins.co.uk/839802